I0668410

THE GLORY OF PAIN

Written By

Corion Gaynes

TABLE OF CONTENTS

THE BOOK INTRODUCTION

The word roller coaster would be the best way to describe my life. Soaking in a memory of heartaches and headaches; I should own stock in Tylenol PM. Wondering will I succeed or fail horribly. The first quarter begins, it was an average fall evening, and disco music was dead. Jimmy Earl Carter was leaving office with Reaganomics starting to take over. But on a lighter note at Harris Methodist Hospital at 2:20 pm an eight pound nine ounce baby boy named Corion Gaynes was born.

The whistle blows my coaches call time out with ten minutes and forty seconds left in the first quarter. My coaches being Hector and Linda Gaynes who fused together a three point play on my very existence to start the game. "Getting at money everyday" I know that this was not grammatically correct but that is what the breakdown of the word Game means.

The second quarter begins as a young adolescent I always felt out of place. I did not walk, talk, or look different; people just never seemed to understand me as a person. After a long day of fighting and being bullied, my life would change forever. Out of nowhere, comes a long pearl white 1987 Cadillac with a diamond in the back, sunroof top, digging in the scene with a gangster lean, ooh, ooh! The doors open and this gorgeous blond bombshell that looked like Farah Fawcett in a platinum chiffon dress with six inch heels, tells me to come here. After walking to the car, a deep very aggressive manly voice speaks out. What the fuck is going on young player?

The person shouting these obscenities was a pimp named Texas Slim. Well damn! of all the people we didn't have a lot of doctors and lawyers in my neighborhood. Texas Slim told me something that I would never forget" Purse First, Ass Last". Always get your money young player. May 20· 1998, senior day at Polytechnic High Schools graduation, the feeling of being an adult comes to mind. Now I have to make some real money because college is not cheap. No one gave me a scholarship so what am I to do? I was a broke, barely educated, young black man, which lead me to start an international escort service. One way to cover up the money that I was making, I got a job working at a five star hotel in the bakery. This turned out to be the best decision because it gave me a career in culinary and the money I had been seeking. This brings us to half time in the game.

THE STRUGGLE

The way we look at each other, is really the way we feel.

This piercing glance on my face as if looks can kill!!

The way we talk to each other.

It's so direct.

Whatever happened to common courtesy and simple respect?

We should let our teachers teach

And our preachers preach.

To where we can endure our obstacles and get to the higher pentacles we plan to reach.

Love thy neighbor like the book of Christ

An untrained mind now who's the real sacrifice?

I really hate myself. Our women love us more.

Obscene words come to mind like bitch and whore

Nobody understands it's a black man's burden to carry.

Maybe because I am physically strong, but mentally weak

Or is it because I choose Ebonics?

Instead of the King's English when I choose to speak.

I really need help. Only we can save me. The nightmares need to stop!

The pain needs to come to an end.

It seems our freedom of expression has turned into a trend.

You take our very soul, and then take our holy soul

And make it into a mantra for your corporate control.

We like gold chains but not master degrees.

Is there even a correlation?

You tell us Nigga please!! You don't need that!!

I take so much from you. And give you little back.

You're not educated, how do know if this change is exact?

My name is The Struggle.

And I come with all of you.

It's your life curse,

So what are you going to do?

Memoir Starts: A Baker's Dozen

1999 I worked in a hotel bakery on the late shift with Ernie a tall white Nazi cheese eating prick from Wisconsin who smelled like feet and farts. Odd characters for some reason always seem to find me. As Ernie and I begin to roll out the dough to make Danish, Ernie turns to me and says they must think I am a white nigger with all of this work.

I tell Ernie no you are a none baking dick head cunt who sticks his fingers in cow's assholes all day. Now shut the fuck up! So we can finish doing our job. Then there was Alonzo and Marcia. Alonzo was a Mex- I- can't not a Mexican from Virginia who transferred to the hotel. Marcia was an Aunt Jemima look -a -like in the flesh. Every time that I would look at her an old Negro hymn or spiritual would come to mind.

One of the things that Alonzo would say to Marcia everyday was hey you big black bitch! Then Marcia would say hey wet back I called immigration for you today. Then there was Tran a Chinese guy who listened to harps and karate kid music all day. Diego was another guy that worked there and he was one of the most influential people in my life. Diego was the man that taught me everything I know about baking besides my grandmother. Cakes, cookies, pies, breads you name it we did it. I am a bad motherfucker when it comes to baking.

Diego was a 65 year old El Salvadorian man who did not speak English, for eight years we worked side by side. This one person has had a major impact on my life. Diego has given me something that nobody can take away and that's a trade and a skill. It just seems that I have to go through the bad people to get to all the good ones.

My thoughts: You may think that I am bashing these people but I am not this was just an everyday occurrence. I learned vital life lessons from every last one of these people. We all can learn something from anybody. This is why I am quick to listen and slow to speak.

PEOPLE WHO MEAN SOMETHING TO ME

Diego: Thank you for giving me a skill that I cannot ever lose. R.I.P.

Memoir Starts: Pimping Is The American Way Of Life

Pimp is such a unique word. Hated by many loved by few. The definition of a pimp on Google and in Webster's Dictionary it is a man who controls prostitutes and arranges clients for them, taking a percentage of their earnings in return. So should I consider myself this word? The word pimp is a noun that is the only thing that's right about this definition.

First of all, I never took a percentage I got all the money. Second controlling another human being has never been a part of my character. Every woman that has been involved with me has done it by choice, not by force. Since the 1970's black exploitation movies have put a negative dramatization on urban life. I guess I am supposed to have a jerry curl and nine gold chains with a peacock colored suit.

Not me sorry folks, but I do not condone this behavior but it's needed. Doctors need nurses, priest need nuns, so hoes need pimps it's just the way of the world. Whoever is reading this is saying that's not necessarily so the woman can do it on her on, and that statement would be true.

Paper in my pocket don't we all like the sound of that. The American economy is based upon a bitch give me my money system. Don't pay your car note bitch give me my money, don't pay your taxes you know what happens Uncle Sam the big pimp sticks his hand out. So don't we all get pimped at one point or another. My primary motivation was the root of all evil at an early age. Why is it rich people have it so good and poor people suffer I find myself having philosophical thoughts questioning God.

Memoir Starts: Infidelity In The Pulpit

Is there a such thing as faith for the unfaithful or are we just fleshly raging hormones with a hard on, is there a limit to the madness. July 20, 2002 stress is mounting because bills are due and things are slow. Mary Jane and I have been getting a little cozy she touched my lips a few times and now I am higher than giraffe pussy. Al Green 's let's stay together was on the radio as I listened to the old school station to try and calm my nerves.

The girls have not turned a date all day and finally the phone rings and it's a trick looking for some companionship. Passion my bottom bitch answers and begins the screening process. She asked are you police officer he said no are you affiliated with any form of law enforcement agency he said no. He asked do you do GREEK" which is another way of saying anal. Passion responded come see me and we can talk about it but not over the phone bring five hundred roses. Passion was a 5,10 caramel tone stallion with the body of an African goddess and lips that could suck better than a Dyson vacuum. Thirty minutes later there is a call on the phone it's the trick and he said he was outside after map questing the directions.

Passion turns to me and tells me to go hide in the back room while she takes care of business. I go into the back room and we play the waiting game. Mentally I imagine the jeopardy theme in my head as I think hurry up and cum and get the fuck out trick. One hour goes by then two I am wondering is Passion hurt or is he still doing his thing, then my phone flashes it's a text message saying I will be done in minute.

The trick finally left and I could come out the back room. Passion picked the money up off the dresser and said here daddy its seven hundred instead of five a smile instantly comes over my face. But she has a look like something is wrong and she said it is. I asked what was the problem did he hurt you and she said no. she asked me do I have a problem with church tides, and I asked what do you mean. She looked at me and told me that he was a Pastor that I just turned a date with and he wanted to pray for forgiveness after the act. I wonder what God would say to something like that.

PEOPLE WHO MEAN SOMETHING TO ME

V.S.: Thank you for giving me a pen and teaching me how to express myself.

Memoir starts: Pimps Gossip More Than Bitches

I35 and Walnut Hill I am standing outside of Denny's chilling. Every pimp in Dallas is up there it seems like. But the hot new topic of the day is one pimp in particular. This pimp was really doing big things. This guy had a black Bentley and a baby blue Rose Royce with the dealer tags on them just to show that the cars were not rented. A few months earlier this same particular pimp had knocked me for one of my hoes. Hey! Sometimes you win and sometimes you lose some that's just how the game goes. It seems skeletons lurk in every one's closet and the pimp with the Bentley was about to get exposed.

The next day comes around and I am back at the same spot. When a pimp name Floss comes up to me and say's man! These streets are getting crazy, did you hear what happen? I respond by saying no what's up? Floss then tells me he was at a hotel on Northwest Hwy with one of his bitches and the pimp with the Bentley had a room next to him. Floss proceeded to tell me that the pimp with the Bentley and another guy from Chicago were fucking each other in the ass.

I bust out laughing and I tell Floss you are a funny dude. He then tells me that he had made ten thousand dollars that night. We shake hands and I congratulate him and I keep going about my way. Later on that night as I am riding in my car thinking it hits me. Floss is from Chicago and something seems a little fishy. Word on the street was that the pimp in the Bentley was a down low brother and he paid Floss ten thousand dollars to fuck him in the ass. Dam! This really fucks me up because I was knocked by a punk pimp for one of my bitches. That sucks! It's certain things that I will not do. I guess money has no sexual preference.

Memoir Starts: The Right Side Of Lipstick

2 o'clock in the morning and Club Lipstick on Harry Hines just closed so you know it's about to go down. At this particular time this is where you would make the most money if you were pimping and hoeing on this track. But the freaks come out at night. Seriously every weirdo that you can think of from molesters, junkies, and dope dealers to sexual deviant tricks roamed in this area. This brings me to the beginning of my story.

Back behind Lipstick is where I would work my girls sometimes; because I could make a few thousand real quick. But on the right side of Lipstick a different breed of animal looms. The animal in question is the transsexual folks! The crazy thing is that at this particular time some of the transsexuals were making more money than the actual hookers. There were unwritten rules, but if you were out there working you knew them.

My hoes pull up one had eight hundred dollars and the other one had six hundred dollars this is a nice start. But it's early so I send them back to work. I get back in my car and look to the right and I see a grey Mustang Cobra pull up. The Mustang has four male drunk white college students. The first place they go is on the right side of Lipstick. The driver of the Mustang sees who he wants gets out of car and then makes a deal with them for sexual services. The other guys in the car walk around the corner to solicit for the same thing.

The night slows down a little bit around about 4:30. A blue Ford F150 pulls up and they seem to be friends with the drunken white boys in the Mustang. The driver of the F150 asks what the hell are you guys doing over here man! The driver of the Mustang response by saying I am getting me some head from this bitch fool! The driver from the F150 started immediately laughing and pointing at the guy from the Mustang. Then the driver of the F150 proceeded to tell him dude you just got your cock sucked by a transsexual.

The driver of the mustang has a look on his face like a motherless child lost in a super market. For the next ten minutes all of his friends continue to clown and make fun of him and then they all leave. 5:30am rolls around and I am sitting on thirty two hundred, so I am getting ready to call it a night. But as I am leaving that same grey mustang cobra pulls back up. I am thinking dam! Somebody is going to make some more money and I call it a night. 6 o'clock the next evening I get a call from one of my close pimp partners. He proceeds to tell me; hey man the track is to hot you may want to move around and work somewhere else. I then ask why!

What is going on out there? My partner then tells me a transsexual had been killed out here; the motherfucker got stabbed twenty times by some trick. Well there goes my easy money for the day. Maybe the college student in Mustang Killed the transsexual I don't know you can draw your own conclusion. I call it the game some people call it life and when something happens like this you have to roll with the punches.

My thoughts : When being a part of this sub culture called the game. You somehow find a way to became numb and oblivious to your surroundings and the things that happen to other people. The way that the transsexual was killed I would not wish that on my worst enemy. The game is a lonely place any sign of weakness and you could lose everything.

PEOPLE WHO MEAN SOMETHING TO ME

Dean: Knowledge at its rawest form. Thank you for giving me a true understanding.

Memoir Starts= You Have A Law Degree But You Want To Be Me

This is totally unnatural that you would find me hanging with a trick. This unlikely event would happen in 2006 after a Dallas Mavericks game. A good friend of mine had introduced me to a guy name Eric. Eric was a short-chubby-dark-haired-thick-bearded-white boy that was a lawyer. By day Eric practiced corporate law for a big firm in Fort Worth.

By night Eric was an Oxycodone pill popping, hoe buying, coke head, gangster rapping wannabe. What makes people want to be something that they are not? After a long night of partying and tricking Eric tells me the next day that he wants me to ride with him. Why not? The guy just paid two thousand dollars a piece for two of my girls.

As we are riding in the car Eric started to play some of the most obnoxious rap music I ever heard in my life. Every word that came out of the guy that was rapping mouth was a curse word. The name of the song was called "I will kill a bitch motherfucker shit". Now I am thinking to myself what in the fuck have I gotten myself into? Riding in a beautiful black on black SLS 550 Mercedes people pull up next to us and give us looks as if we were fucking crazy.

To make matters worse Eric then turns the radio down and says this is me rapping on this song. He then proceeded to tell me that he has a CD coming out soon. Stop the Story! Now this brings me to my point. I would trade every hoe that I ever had to be in this guy's position! Fantasy sometimes can cloud a person's reality.

The stereotypical allure of being someone that you are not could cost you everything. My reality was a living nightmare and the way he was living was the dream of a life time.

PEOPLE WHO MEAN SOMETHING TO ME

Nate: My brother for life. We have been through it all. There are still true friends in this world.

PEOPLE WHO MEAN SOMETHING TO ME

The Fade Em All Click: Cooley, Walk, Tex, Ked: You guys have been there since day one. Thank you for everything.

Memoir Starts: Meth-a-done Misfits

Methadone is a synthetic analgesic drug that is used as a substitute to treat morphine and heroin addiction. It also suppresses withdrawal symptoms and is used as a pain killer. So basically you get off one drug to get hooked on to another one. Whatever happen to just going cold turkey and beating it?

Drugs continue to be a fucked up part of my reality within my inner circle. I am not doing them but Raspberry a red- haired, Peppermint Patty looking white girl and her pan handling boyfriend Jason are. I meet Raspberry and Jason at a hotel that they were about to get kicked out of for none payment. The reason they could not pay was because they had shot up all their money doing heroin. They were junkies but they were nice people that just had problems.

Not only were they using heroin but they were also stealing methadone from the downtown clinic that I use to take them to. Here I am thinking that I am trying to help someone get clean and they are doing this type of bullshit. Man! I can't win for losing. Raspberry finally gets her mind right and decides to come choose up with some pimping. But the only way I could get the money is if her boyfriend Jason could be there to.

What kind of European gay shit is this? I have never heard of a hoe bringing her boyfriend along if she has a pimp. This is just some crazy stuff. But Jason tells me he loves her and he does not mind her doing it. So every time Raspberry turned a date Jason rolled shotgun. Feeding a junky whore's habits has its pro's and con's. The main pro was that if she stayed high she always made money and was willing to work.

Raspberry was a pretty red head that made twelve hundred dollars on a bad day. As fucked up as this may sound I bought a shit load of drugs once a week to keep her high and making money. Raspberry adding to my income was great until the con comes into play. My money started to come up extremely short. Instantly that's a problem. I would never hit a hoe but I would poke bitch in the fucking eye if she had ever crossed me. This bitch was clearly on her way to getting blinded.

Many people have told me that I was a sadistic asshole for my methods of checking a hoe. In my opinion, fuck you pay me to the people who said that. I got issues and I deal with them just fine. The game is a monstrous lifestyle that can sometimes get out of control. In all actuality we all have problems but it seems that us as human beings like to point fingers and not look at our own selves. Money was my addiction. I just wonder is that a problem you can solve?

Everybody has an angle! I have learned that you can't trust a single person in this world! I sit and wonder sometimes who really has my best interest? Between dealing with hoes always trying to pull a fast one on you I can never get I break. I now have to deal with crazy tricks and the police as well. This brings me to my story.

One day in 2006! my escort service got raided by an undercover vice officer posing as a trick. But something was funny about the vice officer he did not arrest any of the girls. Instead he made a deal with them. The officer told the girls that he wanted to speak with me because he had been doing surveillance on me and he knew who I was.

Four girls were working for me at time and three of them told the officer to go fuck his self. But you know it's always a punk bitch in the mix she told him all of my information from where I stayed, to all three of my cell phone numbers. The next day the officer calls me up and say's we need to talk in person. I told him to fuck off because I have no words for the police. The officer then says I want fifty percent of what you make and a free piece of ass three times a week.

After he said that I hung the phone up and started laughing. Two days later as I am checking my mail early that morning. There was an unmarked white Caprice classic outside my house. As I look inside my mailbox there were some pictures and they were of me. The Caprice door opened and it's a short dark-haired Mexican dude with sun glasses on. The dude walks over and say's hey! You like my pictures?

The officer then tells me that he is ready for a deal. Me being the knuckle head asshole that I am, I told him to get the hell out of my yard as I walked back in my house. A week goes by and the money that I was getting from my white bitch in Arlington was coming up short. Come to find out the officer had got to her and was taking the money that I was missing.

Needless to say it was time to do a little of surveillance of my own. The next time that the officer came over I paid one of my partners to follow him and take pictures. The following day my partner has some interesting news for me; he tells me that this asshole is not a police officer. Actually the motherfucker works for a fast food restaurant and then he shows me pictures.

Three days later the now fake vice officer pulls up to my white bitch's house thinking he was going to get some money and some free pussy. Wrong! As soon as he walked in the door two of my partners and I immediately begin to beat the shit out of the guy. As he lie there on the ground bloody and crying the fake officer says you guys are going to go to jail for assaulting a police officer.

One of my partners kicked the fake officer in the ribs and then puts a gun in his mouth. With blood splattered everywhere I tell my partner don't kill him it's not smart. Take his money and identification and then kick him out. One week later the fake vice officer was arrested for impersonating a police officer. This sick fuck had been pulling women over for speeding late at night and then raping them.

My thoughts = I was really reckless at this point in my life. It was like I did not care about anyone seemingly not even myself. This situation could have gone a number of ways.

THE STRATEGY

I am a genius starting a new subculture.

I still want my 40 acres and a mule so I can revitalize agriculture.

All praises to the Supreme Being.

I can understand what you are not seeing.

They even crucified Jesus! We need to learn to please us!

Now your government is passing laws about marrying he/she's!

Your very people are becoming an endangered species!

Satellite's track your every movement through cell phones, cable TV's and burglar alarms.

While secretly they're trying to implant the mark of the beast chip inside of your baby's arms.

By the time I am sixty five I won't have social security!

Because they are too busy spending it all on homeland security!

The only privacy they want you to have is inside of your mind!

That's all they can trust!

Even then if you don't fall in line they will send you to a psychologist!!

My health care is going to stop. Can you please tell me what you are injecting into me from this flu shot??

I see your strategy!! It's abundantly clear!

Drones, terrorists and AIDS, is there anything else left to fear?

Memoir Starts: Bonafide Human Being

Bonafide is considered a term of endearment in the game. In regular life and in the underworld it holds true to its meaning. Defined as sincerely , without intention to deceive in Latin it simply means good faith. This was one of the only things that I was looking for. People think money changes you I seem to think not, money only brings out who you really are as a person. Personally if you were a asshole broke nine times out of ten you will be one rich. This word expresses who I am in adjective form and that's genuine and real.

Memoir Starts: Fat Girls Make Money Too

Society puts a bad image on some things. But it's crazy when you sit and think about it. Why do we as a civilization outcast fat people? This is an error that I have a problem with. In my experience, fat girls cook great food, suck dick, and take care of you a hell of a lot better than skinny girls do. I know that sounds real sexist but that's how I really feel.

This brings one story to mind. I went to the store to buy groceries for my house one day. When I see this voluptuous, pretty full figured woman outside the store. I proceeded to ask her how she was doing and she said not good. Followed by I just got fired from my job and this shit is fucked up! Me being the nice guy that I am, I asked if she wanted a new job and if you do here is my number so call me.

Two hours later my phone rings and it's her telling me to come over to her house and tell her about what I have going on. I get to her house, and she is cooking up a storm as I walk through the door. The first thing out of her mouth is are you hungry and I tell her no but everything smells great. Down to business is what I tell her.

 I run an escort service with several types of clients, are you interested? This is the part of the story where my error comes into play. The first thing out of her mouth is I am too big and I have to pay extra money for my clothes and my airplane tickets etc. Stop the story and go back to my point. Society brings out a low self-esteem in a lot of big people because of the fake weight standards and false images in the media.

I assumed that this insecurity on her behalf, started at a very young age. "Resume to my story" I asked this young lady, had she ever heard of the term BBW? She replied what is that? My response was a big beautiful woman and tricks like big girls too. She then asked what we have to do to get things started. I said to her we need to take some sexy photos and post them on my website so we can have the clients call you.

The young lady says cool and what do I need to wear? I tell her to put on something sexy while I get my camera and laptop. Fifteen minutes later, she comes out in a purple leopard cat suit with six inch heels and a mean push up bra. Pleasantly surprised, I tell her she is going to make a lot of money. She then smiles and says I hope so. After taking the pictures, I grab my laptop and loaded them to my website and a few other escort sites.

 Ten minutes later, her cell phone blows up with clients saying they want to turn a date with her. Like a soldier she goes to work. Her first night working she made a thousand dollars which is pretty damn good! Not too many skinny people have jobs making that kind of money. But some people can't handle making that kind of money and start to do stupid things!

Child protective services did a housing inspection and found crack cocaine then took her son. She told them that she was an addict so she wouldn't get into trouble. When really she was running a dope house and working for my escort service at the same time. Come to find out, she would sell drugs to a lot of the clients that came to trick with her.

Sometimes money is never enough. The last I heard about her was that she had got caught stealing out of the very store I met her in. She was one of the first big girls to ever work for me but she was definitely not the last!

My thoughts: Never judge a book by its cover. Everyone has different taste and sexual preference.

Memoir Starts: In Hot Pursuit For A Prostitute

April 5, 2000 I decided to meet a partner of mine at our local hang out spot. Before walking out of the door I glanced at myself in the floor length mirror . I am fresh dressed like a million bucks. Now it's time to attract a million bucks. Three squirts of CK1 cologne and I am out the door . Fifteen minutes later I pull up to my hang spot Chica's loca's the parking lot was packed so that means this club has the potential for a lot of action tonight.

As soon as I hit the front door I see my partner young Mack with one stripper next to him and another one in his lap with two bottles of champagne . The first words out of his mouth is I just got chose. Then he says man you need to start campaigning these hoes and rightfully so I listened.

The DJ started to play the worse Mexican music I ever herd you know the kind with same beat and a lot of bass. All the girls stop dancing instantly. Now is my chance to seize the moment and survey the room. Gradually I turn into a male lion that's hunting for his pride, I spot a gazelle which is a young twenty two year old light skinned, hazel eyed, big booty woman with a stripper outfit on that says got $.

Hot dam! I am off I walk over with a sense of urgency that you would not believe and say can I speak with you for a second baby doll. She says sure but I am thirsty can you get me a drink. Tell the waitress to make it two. But before I can say one word she asked me how much do I want to spend and can she give me an exotic lap dance. My quick response was hell nawwww ! I am allergic to those and you are barking up the wrong tree for that there is no tricking here. If you are ready to make some real money here is my card call me and then I walked off politely. The next day after a wild night of drinking, campaigning and food truck tacos.

My phone rings but I did not answer because I had a bad hangover. A few hours later I come back to reality and Tammy my BMW (BODY MADE WRONG) bad built white bitch from Kennedale Texas tells me to please answer your phone because it's been ringing all day long. Now I am wondering who the hell keeps calling me from this same number. I call it back and it's the hazel eyed girl from the strip club crying saying she did not make any money last night to pay for her hotel room and can she come stay with me . My reply was bitch I am a pimp you got to pay to play.

Memoir Starts: Turd Flap One Eyed Billie

Las Vegas Nevada, Billie Legler, is in protective custody, waiting to be transported to his new destination. Billie Legler, AKA, Turd flap one eyed Billie, was a college graduate, with a degree in biochemistry. With a resume like this, you were sure that this guy was on his way to stardom. Billie got his nickname because he talked a lot of shit and never kept his mouth closed. Plus the guy was a tall dirty blond-haired stoner that smoked weed all day.

He had a blue eye and a hazel eye, hence the second half of his nickname "one eyed". I met this unlikely character on Flamingo Ave one day when I was trying to make some money. Because the girls I had hoeing for me at the time, wanted to get high. The word on the street was that Billie had the best product for whatever you needed in town.

The girls and I scored an ounce of weed and ten ecstasy pills and kept moving. Billie gives me his number and told me to call him anytime I need something. A few days go by, and I call him up to get some more drugs for the girls and he tells me to meet him at this trailer park on the out skirts of Las Vegas. I finally get there and I am thinking trailer- park-trash-white-boy, typical.

From the outside his trailer looked like it is condemned. Billie invited me in, the inside of his trailer looked like an HGTV interior decorator mixed with an insane chemist had decorated his place. Shocked and appalled I asked him what the hell do you got going on here?? Billie replies all of the drugs I sell to you I make them right here. We do our transaction and I am gone.

Months later I am back in Texas and my phone rings, its Billie checking to see how I am doing. Just trying to earn a living and I am doing well. How about yourself? He proceeds to tell me, that he has a new business deal that he had made. He was approached by the Russian mafia cartel and they wanted him to supply them with Meth and Ecstasy pills. I told him that sounds cool but to be careful with these guys because one wrong move and you can end up dead.

As our conversation continues he tells me that he developed a new form of Ecstasy pill called a Blue Dolphin and he is going to send me some of them to try. In my head I am thinking this asshole is crazy. How in the fuck is he going to do this? Four days later, I receive a white FedEx package from Billie Legler. Shocked and amazed I opened the box and its five bags of skittles in the box. Is this some type of joke I say to myself.

I then opened one of the bags and it's filled with small blue ecstasy pills. Instantly I called Billie and he picks up the phone, laughing and the first thing he says is taste the rainbow motherfucker. Now wire me five hundred dollars before I kill you and started laughing. Then he says just playing, just joking dude. Just consider this an early Christmas present.

I thank him and I got off the phone. Two weeks later, trying to show the same gratitude, I call Billie to tell him to go the Western Union because I was going wire him a thousand dollars just to say thank you. He tells me that he is in a world of shit and to make this the last time that I called his phone. As it turns out, the same thing I warned Billie about came true.

The head of the Russian mafia cartel did not like Billie doing business with no one else. That became a Conflict of interest. So he ordered a hit to be put out on Billie. I never heard from Billie again or even knew his whereabouts. Until one day two months later, I am watching CNBC on TV and they start to talk about a brutal murder involving three undercover cops and another man. They show pictures of the victims and one of them is Billie. The story was reported that they had been bound, gagged, and shot in the head execution style. My mouth drops. My mind draws a blank and a cold damp depressed feeling comes over me.

My thoughts: It took me a long time to come to terms with this. Billie was a real cool guy always full of life and kept you laughing at something. One wrong move and it's over just like that. The lesson that I learned from this situation is that the people you deal with can make or break you. Now I am very selective on whom I deal with.

Memoir Starts: Mixed Emotions

Time mixed with pain equals change that's the equation of life and the radical conversion for the universe. One begins to think when is it enough? Maybe I am addicted to the fast life. The faster the money comes the faster it goes. To this very day I could not tell you where all the money I made went.

My Chocolate Fun

The masses look down upon you for your skin tone.

But when I see you lust comes to mind and your love makes me feel right at home.

Dark as the midnight skies, prettier than the Garden of Eden.

I know the motherland loves you.

But you do have love in this region.

Your inner walls are pinker than raw Filet Mignon steak.

Your waterfalls flow like roaring rapids, my canoe sometimes has to take a break.

You make hair an accessory

Whether you're bald, weave, or lace front, you still look the best to me.

You have more class than a PHD.

All you ever did was trust, honor, child bear, and continue to be a strong woman for me.

Heaven is jealous of you because you took the place of the sun.

The other flavors are tasty

But my preference is Chocolate Fun.

PEOPLE WHO MEAN SOMETHING TO ME

Darene: God really opened up the gates of Heaven when he put you in my life. With you great things are ahead.

THE SURVIVAL

I think I am a little more than a credit score!

If I still don't make enough money what's it all for? You get faulty images from integers

And computer percentages, which allows housing to be a hindrance

Interest rates that make me pay more while

The cost of living in my state pays less.

My blood pressure is so high, because I can't deal with the stress.

Where is my bail out?? I can't even post bond to bail out!! Without you, he, she, and they bringing some kind of doubt.

Under and over qualified for the long haul I applied for twenty jobs to get one call!

And that was to hand out cell phone brochures at the mall!

At this stage you oppress me with minimum wage, as my child support continues to go on a rampage. But I still strive to survive.

Blessed if I made it to 21 and I am still alive.

Hope within takes God, family and education.

Soon before long, I will be the voice of your very nation!

MEMOIR STARTS: WHEN I CAME UP

When I grew up, I got a crash course in life's hard knocks at an early age. At the tender age of eight. My father and mother got a divorce after thirteen years of marriage. It was said that my father was a rolling stone and I am not talking about Mick Jagger.

My parents met at a military social event sometime in late 1970's. When they met, they hit it off instantly. Now that I am a grown man, I look back and think of all the good times and memories we had. I find myself looking at old photo albums, just to relive the more simple times of my life.

My parents gave me the best of both worlds without being rich. The funny thing is that you could not tell me we were not rich. All of my family at that time was so close nit. As far as being wealthy, now that's a different story. 1985, my parents purchased a brand new T-top Camaro and we also bought a house in a nice neighborhood and things were going great. I learned how to fish that year. My father and I spent a lot of quality time together.

But there is always an elephant in the room; meaning some big unforeseen problem. Being a rambunctious kid, I stumbled across something I have never seen before. It was a white powder like substance that I heard grown folks call China. Laughing to myself, as I got older for the longest time, I didn't know that China was a country instead of cocaine.

Cocaine became a fucked up reality for me soon after. My innocence was gone and I began to see what was really going on. My mother and father would probably kill me for writing this shit because it is so near and dear to home. This was the time that I realize, my father was a hustler.

My Thoughts: I got my drive and ambition from my mother. But my work ethic and street smarts came from my father. Both my mother and father taught me how to be a people person and deal with all walks of life.

Memoir Starts= The Hector move

Once a week I make a trip to Dallas to see my father who is my personal barber and plus the haircuts are free. As he cuts my hair we sit up and talk about what's going on in each other's lives. Sometimes we even find ourselves having debates about social and economic norms. Spirituality and man to man talks about women usually make its way into the conversation.

But one particular conversation seems to always come to mind. My father and uncle went back to Detroit to visit the rest of my family because that is their home town. We then speak about my father's glory days and all the wild stuff that he use to do when he was younger. Then he always tells me that I remind him so much of him and we would both laugh.

While in Detroit my father ran across a lot of his old friends from his younger years. One day while hanging on the street corner having a few beers and singing with his friends. An unknown man walks up and he just sits there and watches my father and his friends sing. Five minutes later the man starts to smile and says is your name Hector? My father replies yes who are you? The guy says you do not remember me do you?

My father then replies no. The guy tells my father a story about how one day when he was nine years old. The other kids in the neighborhood were bullying and beating him up. The guy continues by saying my father was walking through a field where he was getting beat up and stopped the fight.

He then says my father told him to come here and let me show you something. The guy said once he got in front of my father he began to demonstrate a fighting move. My father tells him when you fight grab the person behind the knee in a sweeping motion and when the person starts to go backwards, push them with all your might. Now go over there and try it.

The guy said he went back over there and tried it and it worked. From that point on the guy explained how he never lost a fight thanks to the Hector move. The guy then grabs my father and gives him the biggest hug and tells him that he changed his life forever. The guy then looks at my father and tells him that he was his hero.

My thoughts: You just never know how something so small can impact someone in such a major way. Taking the time to show someone a little compassion it can go a long way.

Memoir Starts: What color is my neck

The only thing that I can say about this story is wow! I had to be about eight years old at the time. My cousins and I were at choir rehearsal during vacation bible school. This is when I get called out of my name for the first time in my life. Another kid at vacation bible school called me a red neck, pointy nose, peckerwood.

Then everyone started to laugh and look at me crazy. With me being a light skinned African American male with little melanin in my skin; I really turned red with anger. Plus I had a rash on my neck from poison ivy that I had got from a camping trip. But when I think about it I was a real red neck. Laughing to myself as I got older, thinking damn kids are cruel.

Why do we teach such hatred toward one another? A lot people joke with me saying light skin was in during the late 1980's. But these same people didn't realize I not only dealt with prejudice from other races but my own race as well. Still to this very day a lot of African Americans have a house nigga and a field nigga mentality. Yes nigga, not nigger there is a big difference folks! Anybody can be a nigger, based on the ignorance that they display not just black people. During slavery the more light skinned people were considered house niggers and the darker skinned people were field niggers. White people coined these terms to segregate black people during this era and it seems that this issue is still relevant today.

This complex issue has plagued the African American community since the beginning of time. Where do I fit in? It seems as though I am caught in the middle and my life has always been a struggle. One group of people dislikes me because I am black and my own group of people dislikes me for not being black enough. So please don't judge me for the color of neck because I am not a little kid anymore and you might not like what have to say back to you.

Let us all seek some kind of help for our issues, whether it is mental, financial etc. Because at the end of the day we are passing on deep routed problems to another generation of people that will pass on fucked up disturbing values to another generation. When does the madness end? It must start with you!

PITFALLS

It seems that we all go through different issues at different times in our lives. But the pitfalls for many African Americans, in urban areas are the same. A wise man once presented a challenge to me. That challenge was to look around my neighborhood and see what's wrong and look around a white neighborhood and see what's wrong? The first thing that I noticed was the sale of certain alcohol.

Malt liquor is liquor made from malt by fermentation rather than distillation. In other words, this is a beer with relatively high alcohol content. To make matters worse, it has high fructose corn syrup or corn sugar as it may read on the label, plus dextrose that gives it that fuel like aroma and sweet taste.

In the early 1950's, malt liquors were marketed to middle class white Americans only. The urban community has been the demographic of choice since the early 1980's. This malted poison is no longer sold in liquor stores located in white communities. By selling this cheap bottom of the barrel fermented barley, we continue to keep the poor and lower class at a disadvantage.

Proportion ratios even differ between white and urban communities. The largest serving size of beer that I had seen in the white communities is a 32 ounce can. In the urban communities the largest serving size was a 40 and 62 ounce bottle of beer. Over the years many popular black icons were used to exploit and market the consumption of malt liquor. One has to wonder why you never see certain malt liquor commercials anymore, but you can always see regular beer commercials all day.

Based on my opinion of this pitfall, it seems that people who make these beers only feel that the urban community needs to get drunk quicker. Even though it has not been proven malt liquor consumption can contribute to certain diseases like Gout and Diabetes. This high level of alcohol can lower the PH balance of your body and is characterized by higher uric acid levels.

My Thoughts: Wake up People!! Read the labels of the products that you consume and then do a little research on some of the ingredients. Pay a little more today and live a healthier life. Or go the cheap route and pay hundreds upon thousands of dollars in doctor's bills later.

PEOPLE WHO MEAN SOMETHING TO ME

Harrell: The helpful tips that you gave me are priceless. You are the main person that has always kept me about my money.

PEOPLE WHO MEAN SOMETHING TO ME

My Lodge: Calvin, Satari, Dewayne, Cotton, McKay, Thad, Raymond, Young, Parker, Joe, A. Wilson, Hawkins, Sams: Thank you brothers of the craft. It is truly a new day.

Memoir Starts: Prom queen

High school is a time for learning, book knowledge and life lessons. Between finding your own identity and dealing with puberty we all find a way deal with it. Selena Marquez was always at the fore front of her class. This beautiful, Brazilian and Mexican mix sultry fiery sensation was meant to blossom into something big. After winning prom queen at her senior prom she had to decide what was next for her life. Her mother and father wanted her to go to college and become a doctor. But she didn't dream so big and had no idea of what she wanted to do.

Graduation came and went; now it's Selena first day of college. She is attending a local junior college to get her basic courses out of the way. On the outside Selena had a girl's dream life. But deep down inside is what torments her on a daily basis. When Selena was ten years old she had been molested by her Mother's best friend Julianna and she never told anybody. A social butterfly towards men, but she had an awkward and a bottled up fear of women, that you would have never known.

I finally got my act together and took my ass back to school. This is where Selena and I first met. It was during a lecture in Philosophy class on nature versus nurture where we would connect. It's kind of funny; Selena told me I had a gentle nature about myself. But little did she know that was only in the daytime at school. I was truly an ass hole and I would eat her fine ass up like an American were wolf in London. One day she asked for my phone number out of the clear blue sky and told me to answer when she called. The semester goes by and we got very close but we never fucked.

The next semester starts and Selena is taking classes at a four year college and a junior college. But something is not right with her voice when she calls me. Selena proceeds to tell me that the class that she is taking at the four year college in which one of her professors is Julianna; the lady that molested her when she was younger. Selena continues by saying that Julianna acts like nothing ever happened and she is trying to be cool with her. Mentally unstable, Selena eventually drops out of school.

A year or so later I was at home horny as hell, so I put on a porno movie and started to jack off. Before I could bust a nut I focused on one of the girls in the porno and it was Selena getting ate out by one chick and a dick in her mouth by some dude. My dick instantly goes limp and I turn the porno off.

My thoughts: Selena and I were close friends. I never tried to put her in the game but she ended up in it anyway. Life has a crazy way of working out. I saw Selena years later with another pimp that was from Houston. She could not speak because if she did she would have been out of pocket. But she did smile and wave when her pimp had his back turned. So then I knew everything was ok. Mentally I wish she could have got the help she needed.

MEMOIR STARTS: THE HOLIDAYS

The days of good food and family values are still here. At the age of 11, I could remember my grandmother teaching me how to make her world famous seven up pound cake with butter glaze. As I got older, she started to make me get in the kitchen more and more. The passion for food came alive within me and never stopped.

I got my first cooking job at IHOP when I was only thirteen, because I lied on the application and told them I was fifteen. I bused tables for a while and then I moved up to prep cook months later. After mastering that task, I was promoted to line cook. It seems no matter what holiday that comes around; I can always count on a call from grandma saying we need to get this food together. So what are you going to cook?

Desserts are my specialty because it's something I have a flare for. I tend to leave the cooking to grandma because anybody that has grown up in a southern African American home knows what I am talking about.

Many holidays over the years, I can remember grandma and me slaving in the kitchen for hours upon end to make a bountiful feast. One thing that we can still count on is that if we haven't seen certain family members we will definitely see them around the holidays because of the food. These are some of the feelings I really enjoy. These are the simple things that you don't have to pay for.

My thoughts: My grandmother means the world to me. She never gave up on me even when I was doing crazy things. Without her I don't know what I would do.

PEOPLE WHO MEAN SOMETHING TO ME

Ruth: You mean so much to me. I don't know what I would do without you. Thank you for being patient with me in my growth. No matter what I was doing I always kept God first.

PEOPLE WHO MEAN SOMETHING TO ME

Alexis: Thank you for always having my back. No matter what the situation.

Memoir Starts: When do you learn Humility?

September 18, 2001 its two days before my twenty first birthday and I have big plans to fly to Las Vegas and enjoy myself. Everything was going great, I called Caesar's Palace to book a suite for three nights plus a rental car to move around the city in. Something was wrong this feeling came over me right in the pit of my stomach. Well maybe it's just gas from the pinto beans and cornbread I ate earlier that evening. Two girls that I just knocked from this pimp named Captain brake a hoe called me and said they were going to hit the track and they wanted me to come out there later.

With money on the brain my thoughts were "OK". Seven o'clock rolls around I am on my to check my money because I got three stacks waiting on me. Driving in the car as I am thinking good ole Dallas, Harry Hines Blvd has been great to me. Out of nowhere comes a white crew cab Dodge Ram going full speed to run the red light and hits me head on and I black out. Six hours later I wake up in a bed at Parkland hospital with a torn rotator cuff, fractured leg, and disfigured face on the left side.

Shit!! I have no insurance I feel horrible plus I look like two face off Batman! Where is Bruce Wayne when you really need him? A week goes by and the hospital is looking for their money because I am running up a big bill staying here. So there were payment arrangements made. No one came to see me or even called to check on me. Finally, check out time comes and my mother comes to get me. She takes me over my grandmother's house to where I can have twenty four hour supervision.

Drowning in my own sorrow the feeling of depression starts to creep in and eat away at my soul. What is God trying to tell me? Medication cant heal what is hurting me. Mentally disillusioned with suicidal thoughts tormenting my every waking moment, I swallow five 800 milligram Hydrocodone to finish the pain. The darkest hours are upon me my eyes close and I fade into nothing. A gentle voice that I recognized speaks to me and says time heals all wounds and I am not ready for you to die yet. My eyes open immediately and I am back at the hospital.

Memoir Starts: In my own way

Learning self- worth is sometimes a hard thing. My sub human nature has taught me to be Dr. Jeckel and Mr. Hyde rolled into one. Blinded by the light, like Manford Man I emerged from the dark abyss of hell. Our lowest point in life seems to turn into our greatest strengths. Body building must be in my future for as strong as I need to be.

Memoir Starts: When do you learn Humility? Part 2

Back where I started in this bacteria infested, government funded death trap. As poor as John Peter Smith Hospital's healthcare plan is, I will be dead before I get out of here. Fort Worth's finest and I am not talking about the police force, Ladies and Gentlemen. With breath coming back into my body, the doctor says he is going to make it. They informed my family and everybody rejoices with relief.

But the family next to mine was not so happy. Their son was in the same room, battling cancer, struggling for his life. Matthew Jillian, a high school stand- out basketball player, whose cancer came back once again. Matthew had more livelihood in his middle finger than I had in my whole body. A terminal illness would not keep him down.

After his chemo treatments, we would talk and he always had an upbeat demeanor. He would tell me how beautiful and great life was. We exchanged numbers as I checked out of the hospital. Two days later, October 3, 2001 , Matthew Jillian died. Matthew was my guardian Angel, because he taught me the meaning of life and humility.

PEOPLE WHO MEAN SOMETHING TO ME

Linda: I am in this world because of you. I owe you the greatest thanks. Your work ethic and Love has made me a better Man and Father.

Memoir Starts: Longitude and Latitude

What happens to a person when they have no since of direction but still try to move forward? It's like a tornado hitting a fertilizer factory, shit is everywhere. Do we as human beings know what the right path is? Or is it just a societal standard of what's right or wrong. It is in my opinion that we are all puzzle pieces a part of one big puzzle.

Figuratively speaking, I think God wants us all to come together. Now I am not going to bust out singing we are the world or some bullshit like that, but I do think we should stop and look at the signs. Can you as a person, honestly say that you have done all that you can do? With me maturing and growing more mentally I can say I have.

We as a people need to get back to the more simple things in life and become more at peace. A lot of my selfish ambitions left my mind the day my daughter was born. Karma has played enough cruel jokes on me. I cannot let my fucked up past decisions intervene on her life. Becoming an adult is a state of mind not an age limit. With all of the thoughts that are racing through my head as I write this; one can only pray that I am headed in the right direction.

PEOPLE WHO MEAN SOMETHING TO ME

My Kids: Plain and Simple you are my motivation.

Memoir Starts: What Seems Truly Worth Living For?

What seems truly worth living for? This is the question that has been presented to me. In noun form living means an income sufficient to live or the means of earning it. In adjective form the definition of living talks about being alive and living creatures. My synonym for the definition of living is livelihood. The word livelihood really speaks on the essence of life.

First I have been blessed to even earn a decent living. Not necessarily having my dream job, but as a man I am able to provide for my family. School has definitely become a big part of my life. Having the determination to finish will increase my living standards. Even when I reach a higher plateau I will never get content because of the drive within me. A deep rooted faith instilled in me from birth keeps me grounded.

Second I thank God the Lord of my life every day for being alive. Many people are alive but they are not living. Several opportunities and great things are coming my way in the near future. It seems I just have to be patient and prepare myself for them. Something small as writing this book has given me something worth living for. Writing has given me a positive outlet that I never had. The power that you have in the words that you write is a beautiful thing. When reading them on paper it is like art on a canvas. I smile when I think about being an author. Having a mentor who believes in me even when I did not believe in myself makes a difference. You will always have my gratitude professor! Therapy without seeing a psychiatrist is what I call it. This is truly an empowering feeling to have.

Finally my livelihood is my kids. They seem to motivate me at my lowest point in life. A lot of what I do is for my kids. Passing on certain traditions and teaching them life lessons is a challenge that I am up for. I have become a more responsible person since I had kids. Now I can understand why my parents always told that they wanted me to do better than they had done. It's funny with all the crazy stuff that I have done in my lifetime. One could only imagine! What my kids will do with their lives? Sometimes a person wonders what the final chapters of their life will read. You just never know sometimes with life.

In conclusion I guess it's best to just live and find out as it comes along. Being blessed with life and having the ability to work makes life worth living. With the cold hearted ways of the world that we live in, it's good to see that you can still find genuine people. Human beings that is willing to teach their craft to help educate someone else. "The joys of children laughing these are the makings of you". I am reminded of that old Smokey Robinson song every time I see my kids and that's what truly makes life worth living.

UNDERWORLD GLOSSARY

24/7: Your business is open all night

A brick: A Kilo of cocaine or weed

A stack: A thousand dollars

A Wop: A wad of money

A zone: Ounce of weed

BBBJ: Bare back blow job

BBW: Big Beautiful woman

Bonefide: A genuine and real person.

Bottom Bitch: A Pimp's main lady

Bottom Feed: A man who receives anal sex.

Check: To set somebody straight in reference to doing something wrong.

Cross Country Pimping: Making money all over the country with your girls.

Crow or duck: A black woman in the game.

Doe boy: A dope dealer

Donkey: Big Booty

Dropping an AD: To post an advertisement for sexual favors.

Eggroll: An Asian woman in the game.

Eiffel Tower: Two guys are having sex with a girl at the same time and giving each other a high five.

Finesse Pimp: A Pimp who uses style and grace.

Flat backer: A prostitute that only lies on her back while serving her clients.

Gators: Alligator skin shoes

Getting Chose: A woman or prostitute coming to select a Pimp with money

GFE: Girlfriend experience

Gorilla Pimp: A Pimp that aggressively handles his women.

Greek: Anal Sex

Green: Lame person or a person that don't know.

In pocket: Loyal

Incall: When a client comes to see a provider.

International Pimping: Making money all over the world with your girls.

Jay's: Jordan tennis shoes

Knocking: To take one Pimp's employee.

MILF: Mother I like to fuck

Mitch: A male bitch.

One Shot: Bust a nut or cum

Out of Pocket: Lack of control or discipline

Outcall: When a provider goes to see a client.

Piece: A gun or a man's penis.

Pop: One nut

Rate: How much you charge

Renegade: A prostitute that does not have a Pimp.

Roses: Money

Screening: Check to see if a potential client is cop.

Serving: To call a fellow Pimp

Skittles: Ecstasy pills

Snow or polar bear: A white woman in the game.

Square Business: Real business

Square: A person that is not involved in underworld activities.

Stomp Down: Down for whatever.

Taco: A Mexican woman in the game.

The Blade or The Track: The street or the strip where hoes walk.

Toolery: Tools used to attract a prostitute, such as cars, jewelry, clothes etc.

Trap: A house where narcotics are sold.

Trick Fuck: To pretend to have sex by inserting the man's penis between the thighs and moving back and forth to simulate sex.

Trick: A man who pays for or solicits prostitution.

Tricking your Dick off: A Pimp having sex with a prostitute that is not paying

Two girl show: Two girls doing whatever someone pays for

Working wood wheel: Driving a car with wood grain.

The back of the book

The Glory of Pain

This epic collection of short stories and motivational poems has been put together to form The Glory of Pain. This book talks about the struggles and challenges that Corion Gaynes had to endure growing up on the south side of Fort Worth. These interesting turn of events turned a troubled youth into a positive person in the community. Corion Gaynes is a graduate of Tarrant County College with a degree in Culinary Arts. He is currently furthering his education to become a Clinical Psychologist. The Glory of Pain is the first book of many to come. Thank everyone for reading this book I hope you enjoyed it.

www.ingramcontent.com/pod-product-compliance
Lightning Source LLC
Chambersburg PA
CBHW080842250626
47161CB00009B/3156